2/22

Bernadette Watts, known throughout Europe simply as Bernadette, has illustrated many dozens of folk- and fairy tales. Born in England, she loved to draw from childhood. She studied at the Maidstone Art School in Kent, UK, and for some time was taught by Brian Wildsmith and David Hockney. Bernadette's many beautiful books include *The Snow Queen* and *The Little Drummer Boy*. Bernadette finds her inspiration in nature. Today she lives and works in Kent. She has been illustrating for NorthSouth Books and NordSüd Verlag since the beginning of her career fifty years ago.

VARENKA

told and illustrated by Bernadette Watts

North South

For my Father – B.W.

Long ago a widow called Varenka lived in a little house in one of the great forests of Russia. The house stood in a clearing among the trees where few people ever went.

Inside Varenka had all she needed—there were tables and chairs, bins to hold bread or cheese, and there were shelves to hold the dishes. There was an icon always surrounded with wild flowers. At night Varenka, like all Russian people at that time, slept in an alcove above the warm stove.

Varenka lived contentedly in her house until one morning some people came past and stopped to speak to her. "We are in a hurry," said their leader. "Over there in the west soldiers are fighting and many people are already dead. A terrible war has broken out, and every day the soldiers come nearer. We are fleeing before something happens to us. Pack up a bundle, good Varenka, and come along with us."

Varenka was afraid, but she said, "If I come with you who will comfort the travelers as they pass on their journeys, who will care for the children who wander and get lost in the forest, and who will shelter the animals and feed the birds when winter comes? There is no one here except me, so I must stay. But hurry and be gone, my friends, and God be with you."

So the people hurried on and the widow was left alone.

"Surely I can hear guns and cannons," she said to herself. "Today they are in the distance but tomorrow they will come nearer. What will become of me?"

She bolted the door and closed the windows. As the sun went down over the woods, Varenka prayed to God and said, "Please build a wall around my house so that the soldiers will not see me."

Then it was evening and everything was peaceful. No longer could the guns be heard. Instead, all the birds started singing before they tucked their heads under their wings to sleep. Doves murmured and a nightingale began to chant.

But God did not come and build a wall around her house.

The next day Varenka went deep into the woods to gather kindling. And again she heard the guns in the distance.

"Oh dear," she said. "They are nearer today. What is going to become of me and my house?"

Before nightfall Varenka arrived safely home. An old man was waiting for her. He was all alone except for a small white goat. It was Peter the Goatherd.

"Why are you here?" cried Varenka. "Why aren't you at home with your goats and chickens, your geese and sheep?"

Peter replied, "My cottage is burned down, and the soldiers have taken everything except this little goat who has escaped with me. Please give us shelter as we have nowhere to go, and soon it will be night and wolves will eat us both."

So the widow took in Peter and his goat. She made them comfortable by the stove and gave Peter hot soup to drink. Then again she prayed to God: "Please come quickly and build a wall around my house so that the soldiers will pass by and not see Peter, or the goat, or me."

Then night fell and all the forest was still. The flowers folded their petals together. The small animals that live in trees or in holes in the ground curled up and fell asleep.

But God did not come and build a wall around Varenka's house. The next morning everything was just the same.

The widow went out to search for mushrooms and herbs that morning. Suddenly she came upon a young man sleeping in a hollow tree.

"Wake up!" Varenka cried. "Wake up, now. You cannot stay here or the soldiers will find you. Listen. Can't you hear the cannons crashing in the forest? They are very near."

The young man answered, "Yes, I have come from over there where the war is raging. Everything is destroyed. The land is on fire. I escaped into this deep forest, and now here I am, poor Stepan, with no home except this hollow tree."

"My poor boy," said Varenka. "Come home with me, and I will give you food and warmth."

So Stepan went with Varenka to her house. In one hand he carried a painted picture and in the other a white flower in a pot; he was an artist and that was all he had left in the world.

When the three friends had eaten supper, they said their prayers together, and Varenka said in her heart: "Please God, come quickly and build a wall that is high and strong around my house. Then the soldiers will not find Stepan or Peter or me."

All night long peace reigned in the forest, and the only sounds were the call of owls and the bark of foxes.

In the morning Varenka looked out of the window, and she was filled with fear when she saw no wall had been built around her house.

That day Varenka made the oven very hot and baked bread and cake. While they were cooking there came a sound of weeping from beneath the window, and there outside was a small girl crying bitterly and holding a dove in her arms.

"My dear," said Varenka, "who are you and what are you doing here? Can't you hear the terrible noise of fighting? You should be at home with your parents."

"Oh, dear grandmother," said the child, "I am Bodula Mietkova and I am all alone except for my dove. My mother and father are dead because of the fighting. And now I am running away. But I smelled cake cooking here, and it made me feel hungry."

"Bodula, come indoors. We are a little family here, and now you are the youngest." So Bodula came indoors and she was given cake and tea.

Throughout the day the four friends could hear the guns all around, and they felt that their last day had come. So in the evening Peter played the balalaika and they sang old Russian songs. Varenka could remember her own mother singing those songs over a baby's cradle.

As the day ended and the moon came up the gentle music brought them peace.

That night they prayed all together, and Varenka said, "Tonight, dear God, please build a wall that is so high and so strong no soldiers will see my little house. And then we will be saved, the child with her dove, the artist and his flower, the old man and his goat, and even myself. I am afraid it is almost too late, for tomorrow the soldiers will be upon us and all will be lost."

That night it was very still. And in the most still part of the night came a gentle sound all around the house. Varenka peeped out of the window and saw that snow was falling heavily. It was as high as the windowsill and was still falling.

It fell all night long, deeper and deeper, and at dawn the little house, with all the people safe inside, was quite hidden.

At midday fierce soldiers came by, making a great noise. Inside the house the people were very frightened. And then the soldiers were close indeed to the cottage.

But they passed by without seeing it, because it was so deeply hidden by the fall of snow.

The soldiers went far away and there was no more
war in that part of Russia.

When the snow melted the people came out of the cottage and thanked God they had been saved.

Springtime came. The goat had a kid. The seeds from the white flower grew into fresh new flowers. The dove flew far away to tell the world that peace had returned.

And Stepan, because he was an artist, painted some pictures to tell the story of the wall that was built of snow around Varenka's house.